Sarah Morton's Day

A Day in the Life of a Pilgrim Girl

by KATE WATERS
Photographs by RUSS KENDALL

SCHOLASTIC INC.
New York Toronto London Auckland Sydney

We gratefully acknowledge the following people for their generosity in sharing their time, expertise, and facilities, and for making Sarah Morton's story come alive: David K. Case, Executive Director, Plimoth Plantation; Dr. Jeremy Bangs, Curator; Dr. John Kemp, Manager of Interpretation; James Baker, Director of Research; Elizabeth Lodge, Registrar of Collections; Lisa Whalen, Assistant Supervisor of Pilgrim Village; Sarah Mann, Director of Marketing and Public Relations; Amelia Poole, who interprets Sarah Morton, her family; Regina Scotland, who interprets Julianna Morton Kempton; Jeffrey Scotland; Katherine Wheelock, who interprets Elizabeth Warren, her family; Stuart Bolton, who interprets Goodman Kempton; Peg Golden, whose artistic eye helped me see this story; Sandra Nice, who suggested this adventure. With gratitude to all.

The accuracy of this account has been verified by the curatorial and research staff at Plimoth Plantation.

*For Abigail Hebel Weir who will
lead our family into the 21st century.
—K.W.*

*With love and gratitude to my parents Jean and Jim Carson
and to my friend Thérèse Landry, pilgrims all.
—R.K.*

*For Jackie Duval, my sponsor
—Amelia Poole*

ISBN 0-590-44871-4

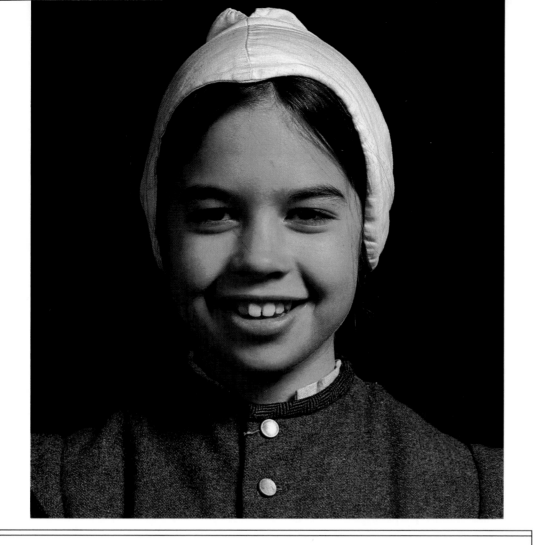

November 12, 1627

Good day.

My name is Sarah Morton.

My family sailed to America four years ago on a ship called *The Anne*. We came to seek freedom from the Church of England. First my family settled in Holland, where I was born. Life in Holland was hard for us, so we set sail for the New World.

My father died that first winter. This spring, Mother married Goodman Kempton. I am learning to call him father and am trying hard to earn his love.

Come thee with me. Let me show thee how my days are.

This is my village.
It is called Plimoth Plantation.

At sunup, when the cockerel crows, I must get up and be about my chores.

I put on my overgarments:

PETTICOAT

STOCKINGS

GARTERS

COIF

APRON

POCKET

PETTICOAT

PETTICOAT

WAISTCOAT

SHOES

and roll my bedding
into the corner.

The fire is mine to tend.

I throw brush on the red coals to make them dance.

Mother and I make the hasty pudding.

I lay the table with clean cloths, bowls, and spoons.

I serve Mother and my new father first. I must stand at my place to eat. Perchance my new father will make a stool for me.

With the table scraps I have collected, I go out to feed the chickens.

Because I have forgotten to latch the pen, I must run our hens a game of chase.

At milking time, I find my best friend, Elizabeth Warren, at the pen. As we milk, we tell each other secrets.

Today I tell her of a dream about my real father. I miss him often, but I do not speak of him to anyone save Elizabeth. I do not wish to seem ungrateful to my new father.

Elizabeth likes to remember the time before she came here to the New World.

She tells me of shops in England full of colored ribbons and of fairs with women dancing.

After milking, I muck the garden to make it rich for planting next spring.

The muck is heavy, and I must often stop to rest. "Hurry along, Sarah," Mother calls from the door.

Oh, marry! I am caught idle again.

I am to pound spices this day.
Our house will have a pleasing scent.
The thump, thump of Mother's churning keeps me company.
I wish I could tell Mother about my dream, but she is quiet today. And I have often enough gotten the rod for speaking out of turn!

Next Mother and I prepare the midday meal.

17th Century Indian Corn Bread

Boil 3 cups of water. Stir in 1 cup coarse cornmeal grits. Simmer until water is absorbed, stirring occasionally. Cool. When mixture is cool enough to handle, turn onto work surface floured with ½ cup fine cornmeal flour. Work into 2 round flat cakes. Bake on floured cookie sheet at 400 degrees for ¾ hour.

(Here is the bread that Sarah made. But it probably would not taste very good to us today!)

When my new father comes home for dinner, he seems pleased with the rich pottage and warm Indian cornbread that we have made!

After dinner, it's time for my favorite task. I draw vinegar to polish the brass.

If I am patient and rub the salt and vinegar slowly, the kettle will truly shine.

Of a sudden, I hear a warning shot from the meeting house on the hill.

It means a ship has been sighted!

Perchance we will have some visitors on tomorrow's tide. I pray that they won't be people who wish us harm.

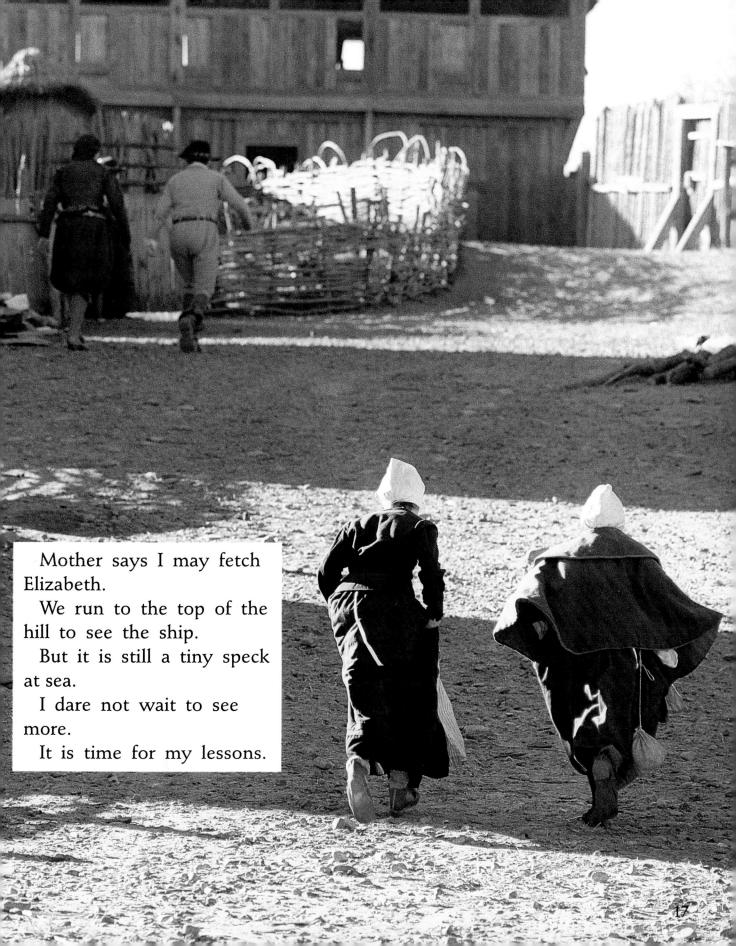

Mother says I may fetch Elizabeth.

We run to the top of the hill to see the ship.

But it is still a tiny speck at sea.

I dare not wait to see more.

It is time for my lessons.

My new father thinks I show a talent for learning!

I am grateful, for in many families girls are not spared from their chores for lessons.

My fingers are clumsy around the chalk, but it gets easier.

Some day I may be able to read Mother the letters she gets from her relations in England!

After the lesson, Elizabeth is waiting for me.
I show her my new father's gift.
He has made me a knicker box!
Elizabeth and I take turns shooting.
We keep score with scratches in the sand.
Today my marbles go through the arches more truly.
Hers bounce back to her.
I am winning, but the sun is beginning to lower
and I must get back to my chores.

I feed the fire to heat the
pottage again, and milk the
goats once more.

The big brown goat is
troublesome.

The more I push, the more
she kicks.

I will have a mark to show
from her tomorrow!

As I return from milking, my new father is coming home.

He has news of the ship.

It carries visitors to our village!

There is much talk about where to lodge them and how to portion out the stores.

After we have eaten, my new father quizzes me on my verses.

I have been learning this one by heart since last Sabbath.

It has words to turn my tongue into a knot.

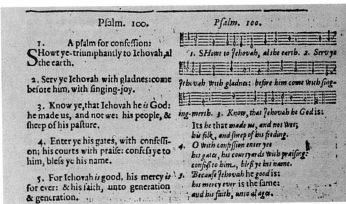

Psalm 100

A psalm for confession:

Shout ye triumphantly to Jehovah all the earth.

Serve ye Jehovah with gladness: come before him, with singing joy.

Know ye, that Jehovah he *is* God: he made us, and not we: his people, and sheep of his pasture.

Enter ye his gates, with confession; his courts with praise: confess ye to him, bless ye his name.

For Jehovah *is* good, his mercy *is* forever: and his faith, unto generation and generation.

This evening Father is pleased with my learning.
He hugs me with pride.
Perchance he does like having a daughter!

Mother calls for me.
We set off for the spring to fetch water for tomorrow.
We look out to sea and see the ship.
Perchance Mother will have letters and a bolt of new cloth tomorrow.

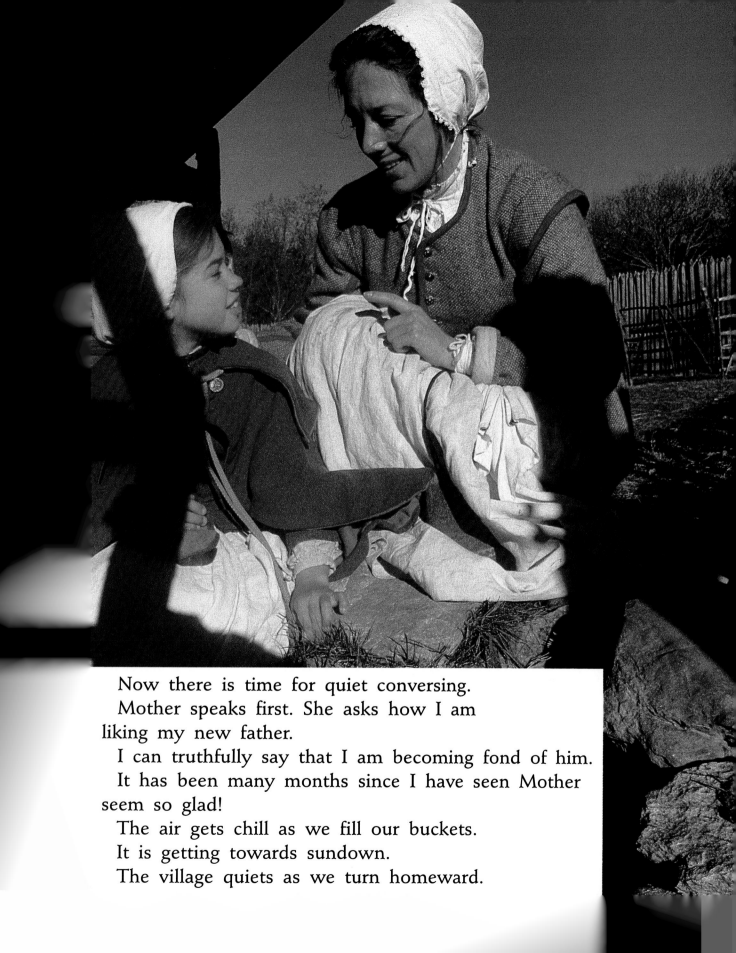

Now there is time for quiet conversing.

Mother speaks first. She asks how I am liking my new father.

I can truthfully say that I am becoming fond of him.

It has been many months since I have seen Mother seem so glad!

The air gets chill as we fill our buckets.

It is getting towards sundown.

The village quiets as we turn homeward.

Father and Mother talk in the candlelight.
I bid them good night.

I get my bedding ready and put my overgarments in the chest.

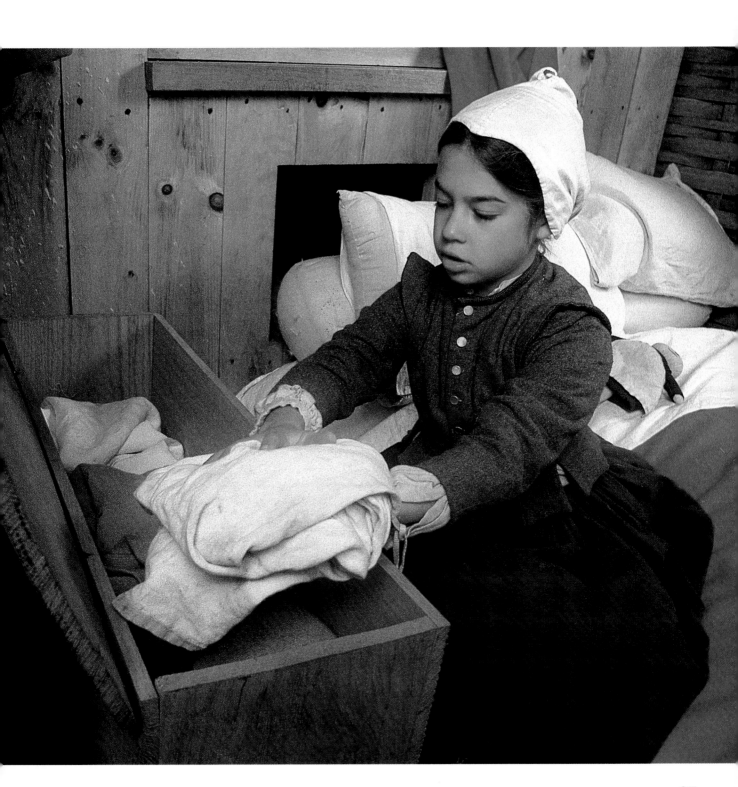

Though I am almost grown, I tell the day's events to
my poppet.

I tell her about the ship in the harbor, winning
knickers from Elizabeth, and my dream.

And best of all, I tell her of my new father's pride in
my learning.

It has been a fine day.

I say my prayers and thank God for his bounty.

Fare thee well.
God be with thee.

About Plimoth Plantation

Plimoth Plantation is the outdoor living museum of seventeenth-century Plymouth, Massachusetts. Visitors may explore exhibits of the *Mayflower II*, a full-scale replica of the type of ship that brought the pilgrims to the New World in 1620; the Wampanoag Indian Settlement; and the 1627 Pilgrim Village. In each of these outdoor exhibits, every effort is made to present an accurate picture of seventeenth-century life.

At the Plantation's Pilgrim Village, the year is always 1627, the date is today's. Almost seven years have passed since the first settlers left the chaos of Europe behind in order to establish their own church and to gain economic prosperity.

The modern visitor may converse with the interpreters as they go about their daily chores, which vary by season. Each interpreter has taken on the role of a real-life 1627 Plimoth resident in dress, dialect, and religious philosophy.

Within the walls of the palisade, rough-hewn and clapboard houses, each with its own kitchen garden, are set alongside an earthen street gently sloping downhill toward the ocean. Animals graze contentedly, and the smell of baking bread wafts through the air. Time is suspended as Plimoth Plantation keeps our early American heritage vibrantly alive.

Notes About the Book

 Who Was Sarah Morton?

Sarah Morton was a real child. She is mentioned in several journals and histories of the period. She was nine years old in 1627.

Sarah's house had a dirt floor and was heated by one fire. The fire was right on the floor. There were tiny windows in the walls with wooden shutters. The windows let out some of the smoke from the fire, but didn't let in very much light. Her house was hot and buzzing with flies in the summer, and dark and cold in the winter. When the winters were very cold, they brought their goats and chickens inside the house to keep them from freezing.

Early settlers didn't bathe as often as we do. Sarah Morton probably had one bath a month during the warm weather, and fewer during the winter. The settlers washed their inner linens frequently, but woolen outer garments were merely brushed clean.

Although Plimoth Plantation is right on the shore of the Atlantic Ocean, people did not swim. They thought that the cold ocean water was bad for them.

When they were very hungry and food supplies were low, they would eat lobsters and other ocean fish. While they were fond of finfish, they really didn't care for shellfish and usually fed them to their pigs!

In the seventeenth century, people did not use forks to eat. If you look at the photograph of Sarah's family eating, you will see that Sarah's stepfather is using his knife to cut and eat the bread. Sarah and her family used their hands to eat food like meat and garden greens. They draped huge napkins over their shoulders to wipe their hands on.

Meet Amelia Poole

When the photographs for this book were taken, Amelia Poole was ten years old and in the fifth grade. She became interested in working at Plimoth because a friend of hers is an interpreter there. Her friend is Katherine Wheelock, who interprets the character of Elizabeth Warren.

Before Amelia began to work in the village, she read books about the period. She was given a dossier to study which included the biography of her family, and information on how to sew, play period games, and how to wear her clothes. Then she was taken into the village to begin interpreting. She spent her days with her sponsor, Jackie Duval, practicing the dialect that Sarah Morton spoke, and learning how to do her chores.

Amelia works at Plimoth three days a week during the summer, and on the weekends during the school year. She spends every day in character, going about her chores in the village. The kitchen garden needs to be planted, weeded, and harvested; animals must be taken care of; brass polished; her house swept; and food prepared.

Twentieth-century visitors wander in and out of the village homes, chat with Amelia, and watch as she goes about her day. Like all the interpreters, she always maintains her seventeenth-century character. Imagine how hard that is when a visitor asks how she liked the TV show last night, or what kind of music she likes!

When asked what her favorite aspects of interpreting are, Amelia mentions the challenge of transporting herself completely into a different time, and the contact she has with visitors from all over the world.

Glossary

I undress and fall into bed. Rachel wakes up and wants to play. I quiet her with one of the songs we sang today.

It was the frog in the well, humble dum humble dum;
And the merry mouse in the mill, tweedle tweedle twino.

Though my hands tingle and my legs are stiff, tis a man's hurts I am feeling. I pray that I will be able to keep up to Father's faith in me, that the rains won't come before the harvest is done, that my snare will catch a fat coney for Mam, and that God will protect us.

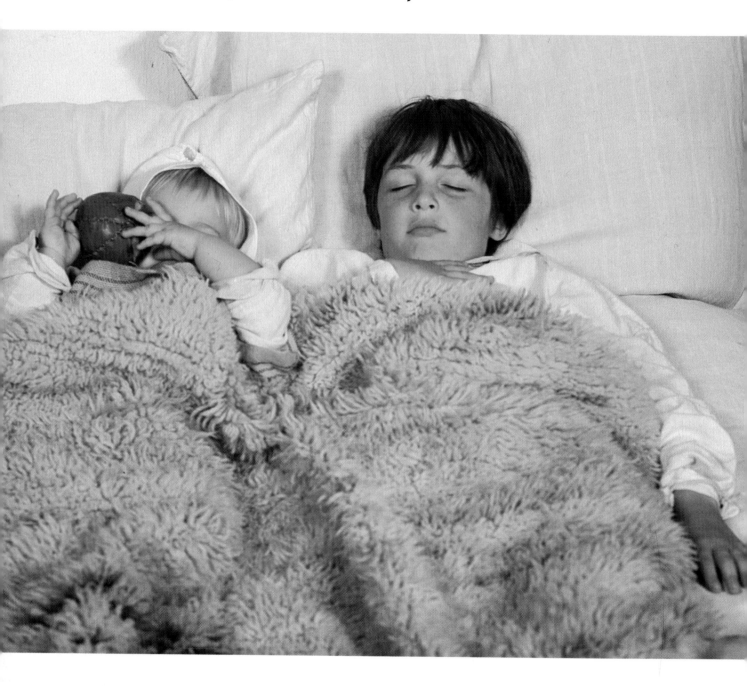

Fare thee well with thy labors.
God keep thee.

The Marriage of the Frogge and the Movse.

Treble. 21. **4. Voc.**

'T was the Frogge in the well, Humble-dum, humble-dum. And the merrie Mouse in the Mill, tweedle, tweedle twino.

It was the frog in the well, humble dum humble dum;
And the merry mouse in the mill, tweedle tweedle twino.

The frog would a wooing ride, humble dum humble dum;
Sword and buckler by his side, tweedle tweedle twino.

When he was upon his high horse set, humble dum humble dum;
His boots they shone as black as soot, tweedle tweedle twino.

When she came to the merry millpin, humble dum humble dum;
Lady Mouse been you within? tweedle tweedle twino.

Then came out the dusty mouse, humble dum humble dum;
I am the Lady of this house, tweedle tweedle twino.

Hast thou any mind of me? humble dum humble dum;
I have e'ne great mind of thee, tweedle tweedle twino.

Who shall this marriage make? humble dum humble dum;
Our lord which is the rat, tweedle tweedle twino.

What shall we have to our supper? humble dum humble dum;
Three beans in a pound of butter, tweedle tweedle twino.

When supper they were at, humble dum humble dum;
The frog, the mouse, and even the rat, tweedle tweedle twino.

Then came in Gib our cat, humble dum humble dum;
And catched the mouse even by the back, tweedle tweedle twino.

Then did they separate, humble dum humble dum;
And the frog lept on the floor so flat, tweedle tweedle twino.

Then came in Dick our drake, humble dum humble dum;
And drew the frog even to the lake, tweedle tweedle twino.

The rat run up the wall, humble dum humble dum;
A goodly company, the devil go with all, tweedle tweedle twino.

About Plimoth Plantation

Plimoth Plantation is the outdoor living history museum of seventeenth-century Plymouth, Massachusetts. The museum portrays life as it was led by the English colonists who came to Plymouth in 1620, and by their Wampanoag neighbors. Visitors may explore *Mayflower II*, a full-scale reproduction of the type of ship that brought the Pilgrims to the New World; Hobbamock's (Wampanoag Indian) Homesite, a re-creation of the lifestyle and customs of the Native People of that region; and the 1627 Pilgrim Village.

At the Plantation's Pilgrim Village, the year is always 1627. Almost seven years have passed since the first settlers left the chaos of Europe behind in order to establish their own church and to gain economic prosperity.

The modern visitor may converse with the interpreters as they go about their daily chores, which vary by the season. Each interpreter has taken the role of a real-life 1627 Plymouth resident in dress, dialect, and religious philosophy.

Within the walls of the palisade, rough-hewn and clapboard houses, each with its own kitchen garden, are set alongside an earthen street that gently slopes downhill to the Atlantic Ocean. Sheep, goats, and cattle graze contentedly; chickens, roosters, and cats wander in and out of houses; and the smell of baking bread and bubbling fish stew wafts through the air.

Time is suspended as Plimoth Plantation keeps our early American heritage vibrantly alive.

Mayflower II

Notes About the Book

Who Was Samuel Eaton?

Samuel Eaton was seven years old in 1627. He and his family sailed to the New World on the *Mayflower*, the first English ship to bring colonists to Plymouth, Massachusetts. The Eaton family came to the New World for economic reasons, not for religious ones. They were probably originally from Bristol, England.

The *Mayflower* landed first on Cape Cod, but the travelers didn't find a suitable place for a settlement so they continued to Plymouth. Because it was winter and the Pilgrims had to build houses to live in, many spent most of the winter living on board the ship. More than half of the passengers, including Samuel's mother, died that first winter of overexposure to the cold, and inadequate diet.

Samuel's father, Francis, was a carpenter. He traded his skill for goods, and the family was neither the poorest nor the richest in the village. Samuel's father remarried, and Rachel was born. In the years after 1627, Samuel's stepmother had two more children.

Samuel grew up and apprenticed for seven years in husbandry, which is farming. Then he married and had his own farm, first in Duxbury and then in Middleboro, Massachusetts. Samuel married twice and had six children. The four about whom there are records were named Sarah, Samuel, Mercy, and Bethiah. Samuel lived to be 64 years old.

Meet Roger Burns

Roger Burns was seven years old in the summer of 1992 when these photographs were taken. He was about to begin second grade. Both of Roger's parents are descendents of *Mayflower* passengers. And they still live in Plymouth! Roger's mother is an interpreter at Plimoth Plantation, so although Roger does not yet work at the Plantation, he is familiar with the village and many of the staff.

Looking back on the week of taking pictures, Roger remembers that the clothes were very hot and the water pail was very heavy. He particularly enjoyed being photographed with the baby. Roger would sing songs and make noises to keep the baby entertained. He also liked the lunch shot because, for the first time, he discovered that he likes Dutch cheese!

Roger hasn't decided what he wants to be when he gets older, but he says that he has learned a lot about patience from working on this book. During the long waits while the photographer set up the lights and the museum staff checked the setting, Roger played electronic games, learned how to make a blade of grass whistle between his thumbs, and rounded up hens and roosters.

Sowing

Reaping

Binding

About the Rye Harvest

The Plimoth Plantation settlers brought many seeds with them from England. They did not really know where they would settle, and so they didn't know what kinds of plants they would find. In 1627, the villagers were growing Indian corn, which was a native plant, and barley, wheat, and rye from seeds originally carried from England. They used Indian corn to make flour, and traded it among themselves for other food or services, such as blacksmithing and carpentry. They also traded corn for fur with the Native People to send back to England to pay taxes to the English investors who put up the money for their voyage. They used barley to make beer, and wheat and rye to make flour for bread, pancakes, and pastries.

Rye seeds were usually planted in September, although occasionally they were planted in early spring. When the rye was ripe, it was cut and bound in sheaves. The sheaves were stacked together in shocks and left in the field to dry. Then the men threshed the rye. They beat the stalks so that the tiny grains fell out. Next the women winnowed the grain outdoors to remove the thin covering around the grain. (The covering is like the skin around some peanuts.) They put some grain in a wide, shallow basket. Then they tossed the grain up in the air. The grain kernels fell back into the basket, and the coatings blew away in the wind.

Women and children then ground the grains into flour using a mortar and pestle. Usually people made only as much flour as they needed, and kept the grain stored in barrels or sacks. The straw that was left behind from the threshing was used to thatch roofs, to stuff mattresses, and as bedding for their animals.

Threshing

Winnowing

Grinding

Glossary

Bandolier — a strap worn across the chest to carry vials of gunpowder.................... 30

Bind — to tie 16

Bootless — groundless, useless... 18

Breeches — knee-length pants ... 6

Coney — adult rabbit 9

Curds — a soft cheese that hasn't been pressed or aged, such as cottage cheese 29

Dally — waste time, dawdle..... 14

Done — tired out 22

Doublet — jacket................ 6

Fetch — get 8

Folly — foolish 18

Gammy — clumsy.............. 8

Garters — bands used to hold up stockings 6

Ground — fields 10

Hone — sharpen 23

Lest — in case 7

Lief — rather 10

Long clothes — long, dresslike clothes worn by young boys and girls until they were five or six years old.............. 8

Morn — morning.............. 7

Mussels — edible shellfish....... 26

Narry — not 18

Naught — nothing.............. 14

Points — strings used to lace doublet and breeches together.. 7

Pottage — thick stew........... 9

Reap — cut 10

Rye — a cereal grass whose seeds are used to make flour .. 3

Samp — cracked corn cooked to a mush 13

Sickle — a tool with a curved blade used to cut grain stalks... 16

Slack — lazy or forgetful 14

Smart — hurt 22

Snare — a rope trap for catching animals 9

Spring — a pool of fresh water that comes from the earth..... 8

Stockings — long socks 6

Stores — supplies of food 14

Straw — stalks seeds grow on... 18

Sucking child — nursing infant.. 3

Upgrown — grown-up........... 13

Watch — guard duty 30

Weary — tired 29

Wee — little or young........... 3

Wield — use 16

40

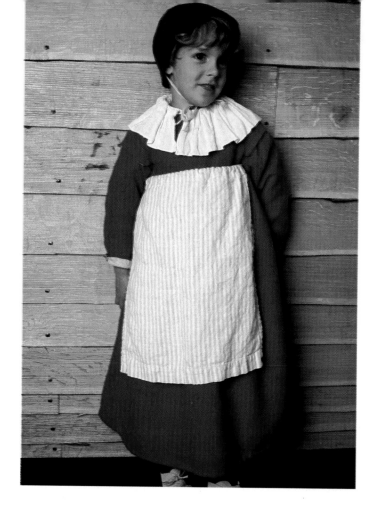

Of Long Clothes and Breeches

In the seventeenth century, both boys and girls wore dresses until they were six or seven years old. Dresses for very young children had strings attached to the backs of them, called leading strings (*see page 20*), so that a parent or an older brother or sister could keep the child from falling down while he or she was learning to walk. When a boy was about seven years old, he got his first pair of breeches. Boys looked forward to wearing breeches because it meant that they were almost grown.

The Wampanoag People

Wampanoag means "Eastern people." The Wampanoag and other Native Peoples shared the land we now call Massachusetts. They hunted and fished and farmed. The Native Peoples had been trading furs with European traders for years before the *Mayflower* landed. But the *Mayflower* brought the first group of European people who would settle permanently on Wampanoag land.

The women Samuel greets in this book are wearing a combination of Wampanoag and English clothes (*see page 26*). They got the English clothes either as gifts or by trading. The red blanket was worn like a shawl for warmth.

cold ocean water was bad for them.

When they were very hungry and food supplies were low, they would eat lobsters and other ocean fish. While they were fond of finfish, they really didn't care for shellfish and usually fed them to their pigs!

In the seventeenth century, people did not use forks to eat. If you look at the photograph of Sarah's family eating, you will see that Sarah's stepfather is using his knife to cut and eat the bread. Sarah and her family used their hands to eat food like meat and garden greens. They draped huge napkins over their shoulders to wipe their hands on.

Meet Amelia Poole

When the photographs for this book were taken, Amelia Poole was ten years old and in the fifth grade. She became interested in working at Plimoth because a friend of hers is an interpreter there. Her friend is Katherine Wheelock, who interprets the character of Elizabeth Warren.

Before Amelia began to work in the village, she read books about the period. She was given a dossier to study which included the biography of her family, and information on how to sew, play period games, and how to wear her clothes. Then she was taken into the village to begin interpreting. She spent her days with her sponsor, Jackie Duval, practicing the dialect that Sarah Morton spoke, and learning how to do her chores.

Amelia works at Plimoth three days a week during the summer, and on the weekends during the school year. She spends every day in character, going about her chores in the village. The kitchen garden needs to be planted, weeded, and harvested; animals must be taken care of; brass polished; her house swept; and food prepared.

Twentieth-century visitors wander in and out of the village homes, chat with Amelia, and watch as she goes about her day. Like all the interpreters, she always maintains her seventeenth-century character. Imagine how hard that is when a visitor asks how she liked the TV show last night, or what kind of music she likes!

When asked what her favorite aspects of interpreting are, Amelia mentions the challenge of transporting herself completely into a different time, and the contact she has with visitors from all over the world.

Glossary

Bedding—Mattress stuffed with straw 7

Churning—Making butter by hand 13

Cockerel—Rooster 6

Coif—Tight-fitting cap 6

Conversing—Talking 25

Fetch—To get 17

Game of chase—To run to catch something 9

Get the rod—To be punished . . . 13

Good day—Hello 3

Goodman—Mister or Mr. 3

Hasty pudding—Oatmeal or cornmeal cereal 8

Knickers (ka-NIK-ers)—Marbles . . 19

Mark—Bruise 20

Midday—Noon 14

Muck—Fertilizer made with straw and animal droppings 12

New World—What America was called by explorers and pilgrims . . 3

Of a sudden—All at once 16

Oh, marry!—Oh, no! or Oh, gosh! 12

Out of turn—At the wrong time or without permission 13

Overgarments—Clothes 6

Perchance—Maybe 8

Poppet—Doll 28

Portion out—Divide 21

Pottage—Thick stew 15

Sabbath—Sunday or the Lord's Day 22

Spring—Well or brook with fresh water 24

Stores—Supplies of food 21

Task—Chore 16

Tend—Take care of 8

Thee—You 3

Truly—Accurately 19

Waistcoat—Vest or jacket 7